one note symphonies

Books by Sean Brijbasi

Still Life in Motion
One Note Symphonies

one note symphonies

Pretend Genius Press

London, New York, San Francisco, Seattle, Washington D.C.

www.pretendgenius.com

Published simultaneously in the United States and Great Britain in
2007
by Pretend Genius Press
London, New York, San Francisco, Seattle, Washington D.C.

Copyright © Sean Brijbasi

ISBN 978-0-9778526-8-0

contents

for Emma

diary of a composer:
a one note symphony

diary of a composer: a one note symphony

blue balloon

Malene rests on her back with her right leg pointing toward the wooden ceiling. A blue balloon descends on her from a hanging stained-glass lamp, and she raises her right arm, then spreads her fingers to push it gently away. She glances at you and turns onto her side.

Your eyes move casually from her breasts to the book you are reading, and the blue balloon waits for her to roll onto her back again before falling towards her face.

The first novels you read to her were westerns, during which time she wore cowboy hats and boots, and once even a full Indian headdress. Then you tiptoed on to romances, but skipped the details of seduction, leaping over paragraphs with a simple "they went into the bedroom and closed the door." You were terrified.

It was only recently that you stumbled upon the courage to read the more amorous, even erotic narrative, and began adding details, lengthening sentences to a few paragraphs, and paragraphs to a few pages, with the result lying comfortably naked before you.

You cross your legs (thin pants) to hide your growing erection, and continue reading where you left off.

diary of a composer

...I whispered 'hello' into my cigarette and exhaled, guiding the smoke towards a woman sitting at one of the front tables. But my message reached a man only two tables away who turned and smiled.

"Not you," I said, shaking my head.

The man sneered and looked away. The band was taking the stage when I took my trumpet from its case, stood on my chair and played one note, holding it for as long as I could. People glared at me in amazement. Napkins were beginning to rise from the tables, but I was interrupted by two waiters who stomped toward me.

I jumped down from the chair, took a quick bow for my appreciative audience, and left the small café, my trumpet's one note (h flat) still buzzing in my ears.

You see music lover, I have spent my whole life composing a symphony, and have written one note, one perfect note...

a dolphin passing

...the Palae Bar on Ny Adelgade was filled with people. Outside, animals crowded the windows: dogs, cats, birds of every kind. Someone screamed (jerking his hand back and forth like a woodpecker) he saw a dolphin pass by, but no one turned to look--Cæcilie was singing.

'...no time for chittin' and chattin' and chittin'...'

(cue piano solo)

The dolphin was me, and it is peculiar that someone mistook me for a dolphin, because there really is no resemblance (other than the glossy, wet look of my skin). I don't like swimming, unless the water is deep--ocean deep, and even then it's only the sensation of floating from bottom to top that I relish. The act of swimming itself never appealed to me. (In fact, between you and me, I don't know how to swim, and have never been near an ocean my entire life)...

(piano fades, cue drum solo)

4

a flying rook

...the dull brass of my trumpet reflects a rising sun in my opening and closing eyes. I have a frightening secret to tell you music lover, prepare yourself.

(drum roll, the sound of thunder)

It is I who make the sun rise, and if I so desire, can make it stay fixed in the sky for as long as I play my symphony. Modestly stated, I am the most dangerous human being in the world, for I fear (with practice) that I could make the sun rise so high it would disappear; its rays wouldn't reach the Earth and everything would be in darkness.

An old man in a nearby balcony appears moments after me and I free one hand from my trumpet to wave to him, but he doesn't wave back. It is the same every morning.

After raising the sun, I walk to Amagertorv and play my symphony over and over again until darkness falls. Three drunks throw bottle caps in my hat; others toss me a few kroner. I'll admit it is a meager amount, but I don't leave discouraged (what is money to me?). Throughout the day I feel the wind picking up, and witness with my own eyes, hats flying from heads, and a chess piece (a rook I believe) rising towards a broken tree limb...

a torn page

You glance over the books on the shelf in search of a novel that will help you take the next step with Malene, and you finger de Sade's Juliet, but move on. (A well-planned step remember, not a reckless leap.)

Your eyes work backward to P, Paya, Señor Oneypa Paya, and you pull out the master's latest work (Don Quixote's Map of the World), an erotic expedition of the female body. You browse through a few pages when you notice a piece of paper trapped between the books and the shelf. You see what's written on the paper and gasp (actually gasp) in amazement.

"What does it say?"

You don't answer, but look to see if anyone is watching you, then hide the paper under your jacket. You flip conspicuously through Paya's novel, replace it on the shelf, and leave the bookstore.

windmills

If Don Quixote were to mount his pitiable steed Rocinante and go in search of adventure today, he would be arrested for trespassing. His map of the world has changed from vast spaces and open fields to the naked body of a woman--a frontier as ambiguous and complex as Don Quixote's.

But I can't believe that you, faithful reader, are still searching for adventure. Together, you and Malene have visited Dodge City, Paris, St. Petersburg. You have fought bandits, married, divorced, bore children, honeymooned in Singapore, had affairs, grew old, and even died together. But when Malene smiles, you wonder if it is a smile at all; if her hand caressing the sofa is a flirtatious intimation of things to come between you or just capricious housework? Are those giants or windmills off in the distance?

(Speak philosopher...)

It isn't adventure you're searching for dear reader, but certainty. The certainty of a smooth, heavy stone in your hand, or of a dense book. You can be certain of those things. You feel their weight. But you can't be certain about a strand of a woman's hair, or of a woman's love. Such things lack the weight of certainty. They float away, vanishing like words read from a page, specters of an already grasping memory.

I have come to the conclusion that you aren't acting like a man at all (vacillating, rationalizing, procrastinating). You aren't like the characters in the novels you read to Malene, and don't dare attempt an assault on those delicate borders I have established between you two.

However, we grant you some reprieve, for you were last seen (good eyes Sancho) mounting a horse, grumbling in a voice that was hardly your own, about giants somewhere in the distance.

unmeasured sky

...I am on a ferry crossing the sound to Malmö. The sun beams down on me. Earlier this morning, for the first time in my life, I woke up late. I thought of the confused, certainly terrified people in the world who expected sunlight already. But when I rushed out onto my balcony, I realized the sun was making a rapid ascent without me. It was I who became confused.

I couldn't believe my symphony was being performed without me. Yet, before my disbelieving eyes, a red-orange note scaled a barless, unmeasured sky.

I gave my trumpet a suspicious sidelong glance to which it responded with a sinister gleam. (I had sensed in the last year or so a growing ambition in the devious horn.)

I grasped the situation immediately and struggled to hide my feeling of panic, smoking a cigarette, walking around the room, speaking as if to remind myself of plans made for the rest of the day.

Then, like a sudden fortissimo, I charged the unsuspecting instrument and locked it in its case. I decided to get rid of it, but quickly, before the sun disappeared forever. I went to a pawnshop and traded in my hat for another trumpet.

Don't worry music lover, I am the near antonym of stupid. I realize just as you have (you have realized it haven't you?) that if I simply throw the trumpet overboard, it will make itself float to the surface. Even sealed as it is now, it still raises the sun higher and higher.

I will take the twisted brass into the sound myself and anchor it somewhere deep, where its diabolical rendering of my symphony will be muffled forever. Then I will play my h flat symphony on my new trumpet and float safely back onto the ship. Tomorrow I will raise the sun as always, wave to the old man, then walk to Amagertorv.

But before I go music lover, I must confess that for a brief moment this morning, hidden in the shadows of panic and fear, a feeling of relief gripped me. The sunrise is a great responsibility...

the heaviness of love makes blue balloons float

You dismount and walk into the room where for the last year or so you have read to Malene. She sits naked on the couch, playing with the blue balloon, and you sit beside her. She is startled.

8

"Isn't he going to read to me?" she asks.

"I don't know," I reply.

"Yes," you say.

You look down at the solitary piece of paper you found at the bookstore and lean over to Malene, singing into her ear.

"Again," she says breathlessly.

You take a deep breath, and once more sing into her ear (this time the left one).

Malene puts her arms around you and pulls you on top of her as she kicks the blue balloon away and watches it float outside the window. You relish the heaviness of your own body lying on top of hers as you tear the page into pieces (pieces I try in vain to collect), humming over and over again, softer each time, into her ear.

Malene brushes some lint from the sofa's arm with her free hand. (revenge of a jealous author)

the old man waves

...you didn't think you would hear from me again, did you music lover? But here I am, and here is what happened--*sans drame ou melodrame.*

I forced the treacherous instrument under a large rock near swaying kelp, then put the new one to my lips. I closed my eyes and played my symphony, holding it longer than I had ever held it before, and felt a rush of water and air surrounding my body. When I opened my eyes, I saw København below me. Around me, there were fish, hats, picnic benches, people, bicycles, people on bicycles, circling passing clouds.

A blue balloon drifted to and fro and I grabbed it by its string (I have it in my hand even now). I saw the old man with his feet pointing toward the sky, clutching the railing of his balcony with both hands, and I waved to him. He released one hand to wave back, and the other hand slipped and he floated away.

My tears float as well music lover, because I am sad to tell you that my diary has come loose in this wind, and the pages fly about like leaves. I must find them, because my symphony (my life's work!) is written there, and strange as it may seem, it has--*absolument*--vanished from my memory...

the portrait

the portrait

the girl cries

Martin followed the thin lightnings of blood from her pupil to the inner corner of her eye, where a wave pushed gently behind the soft white wall before emerging as a single oblong tear gliding down the crease of her nose. It continued to her lip, then vanished into the tip of her tongue, leaving its winding trail behind. Martin wished to taste it also, and for a moment (an eternity in the lifetime of a single tear), it was all he imagined. It could easily be done he thought--simply direct its delicate flow onto his finger as he dried her face, then unobtrusively absorb it with his tongue. With his slippery, pointed tongue, Martin wished to sample the sadness of the girl's soul. That oblong tear framed by the girl's blushing flesh was beautiful--not just the tear, but the entire image--and Martin wished to know what thought inside the girl's head was artist enough to create that image.

the girl stops crying

No more waves pushed against the white wall, and the winding trail dissolved into the girl's skin. It was only when she opened her mouth to speak that Martin saw her face as a face, as the face of a human being in despair for the first time, and wondered why, why was she crying? It wasn't the kind of thing one expected to see when just arriving at a party.

"What is it? Are you okay?" he asked, putting down his coat. His questions treaded lightly over her sobbed, meaningless utterances.

The words she used were starting to sound familiar, a few even had meaning, but it was difficult to hear her above the chatter and music filling the tiny apartment, and Martin pulled her away to the hallway by the closet.

"Here, now we can talk," he said putting an arm around her. "You'll be fine."

She started again, her frustration bursting forth in tiny droplets of sweat around her neck, and Martin (in a gesture that was neither awkward for the situation nor unfaithful to his character), put his arm around her back and pulled her close to comfort her. He passed his hand over her face, but her cheek was dry. Even the thin lightnings of blood had disappeared, having retreated into her skull.

"Are you okay now?" he asked.

"Yes," the girl said.

"My name is Martin," he said, and leaned his head against hers, but she pulled abruptly away from him.

"I'm fine now," she said, and walked away.

the girl laughs

From across the room of flashing lights and dancing bodies, Martin watched the girl's face. Now she was smiling, what more, laughing--a sincere, full-bodied laugh that came from the pit of her stomach. Laughing, the girl was ugly. Didn't she realize this? Didn't she ever see herself laughing in a mirror? There was no one uglier in the room when she opened wide that hole in her face, showing teeth, twisting cheeks, and cackling, a cackle birthed from the inner twistings of her intestines. Martin imagined that when someone told her a joke, it was only to see her face twisted into a laughing display of ugliness and make the joke doubly amusing. It grieved him to see her in this way, for it clashed with the image of her already formed in his mind, the beautiful image of one large oblong tear surrounded by blushing flesh. He had felt her flesh with his own fingers, with his own flesh, which made her more real to him, made the distance between them nil, and it seemed as if he was touching her from across the room.

the photographs

A heavy hand hit Martin's back, and he struggled to swallow the rum sliding by his trachea.

"How are you enjoying the party?" the voice came from beside him.

Martin's eyes left the laughing girl and followed the hand reaching out to shake his, from wrist to elbow, up to shoulder, neck, and finally face. It was Tom.

Tom wanted Martin to paint a portrait of his sister as a surprise birthday present, and in order for Martin to get the flavor of her personality, invited him to observe her at the party. Martin wasn't sure, however, which girl was Tom's sister.

Tom reached into his pocket and pulled out five photographs. Martin was startled by what he saw. There before his eyes was the same girl who became ugly when she laughed, and in every photograph (although desperately camouflaged by shadows, twitches, waving hands, and hair) she was laughing.

"Don't you have any others?" Martin asked.

"Yes I do," Tom said. "But I want a portrait of her laughing. I want her to be happy. I want her to be seen as the happy person she is."

Martin wanted to know if Tom had ever seen his sister with a tear gliding down her cheek, a tear surrounded by her blushing flesh. If he had seen that image of his sister, Martin thought, he would have ripped those photographs he gave him into unrecognizable shreds, hoping they could never again be pieced together.

the suicide

Martin sat alone by the window. He really didn't want to paint a portrait of the girl laughing. He shuffled through the photographs, and a breeze lifted one of them from between his fingers, carrying it out into the night. It hovered upright in the air like a meditating diver on a diving board.

Martin felt the girl's fingers sliding between his (the same fingers violated by the thieving wind) and turned to find her in the crowd. She was in the center of a small circle of people, and had suddenly opened wide that hole in her face, showing teeth, twisting cheeks, and cackling, a cackle birthed from the inner twistings of her intestines. It looked as if she was screaming, as if she sensed the approaching death below, and Martin, feeling her fingers as though they clutched his, turned in a panic towards the open window.

He reached for her, but she was beyond him. Their fingers unlocked, and his remained outstretched, while the photograph hovered upright in the air like a meditating diver on a diving board, then plunged twelve stories, fluttering back and forth, connecting smile after smile, before finally reaching the sidewalk.

The girl suddenly closed that hole in her face, betraying the desired expression of her intestines. Her face took on the features of a corpse made pretty for the coffin, while the faces around her continued to stretch and wrinkle with unrestrained laughter.

Yes, Martin thought, the image of the girl with her distorted laughing face was still with them, and would still amuse them long after she, her face, her body, disappeared from this world.

the immortal ugly

It was unfortunate that long after the girl becomes merely an apparition of memories, her portrait will hang above a fireplace or by a bed-table as the treasured keepsake adding substance to that slowly fading ghost. She will never close that hole in her face, for long after death's authority commands that she stop laughing, she would continue laughing (having found a loophole in the portrait) and therefore remain ugly.

There were probably two or three hundred pictures of her laughing. Why did her brother wish to add a painting to the lot? People would see her portrait and wonder why someone so ugly was the subject of an artist's canvas. In a figurative sense of the word, her ugliness would become immortal.

the girl goes to her car

At one time or another, everyone approached Martin about the portrait Tom asked him to paint. They all wanted a part in choosing which of the photographs should be his model, and soon Martin simply distributed the photographs amongst them. When the laughter became too distressing, he rested by the window.

Down below the girl was walking to her car. She suddenly stopped, bent over and picked something up from the sidewalk. She held it out away from her face, moved it closer, then moved it away again. It was the photograph.

There it was. And that is important, Martin thought. There it was. Not in the controllable environment of a personal photo album or a desk drawer, but outside where she had no control over it whatsoever. It was her lucky opportunity to steal a glimpse of her fate, but the circumstances did not permit it. She could only wonder what her photograph was doing on the sidewalk, and nothing more. She didn't see herself in a strange environment beyond her control.

She shoved the photograph into her pocket and continued walking. She reached a blue car, opened the door and sat in the driver's seat. Ten minutes later, she reopened the car door and walked back to the apartment, glancing up at the window for only a moment. Martin could barely see her face, but he knew she had been crying.

the attempting comforter of her melancholy

Martin believed that it must have become increasingly difficult for the girl to control the thoughts inside her head. It would take little, perhaps something as little as a gesture to bring them out again.

What did she know of Martin? Nothing. He was only a stranger who happened to witness the single manifestation of her distress. The only memory of him was that of an attempting comforter of her melancholy. In her life, he occupied no other place. In fact, not only did he occupy no other place, but he triggered only one memory. Nothing about him--his large eyes, his hands, the way he spoke, the sound of his voice--remotely reminded her of anyone or anything else. The only memory connected with him was the one artist enough to create the image of her tear surrounded by blushing flesh, the one he knew nothing about. But did he really need to know?

A woman walking up an escalator puts her index and middle finger into motion upon the rubber escalator handle, having them walk parallel to her. Another woman she has never met sees this child-like gesture and it reminds her of a little boy whose fingers walked similarly along a wooden beam at the airport where she was saying good-bye to her lover. The woman going up the escalator has no idea how painful it is for the other woman to see her fingers walking in such a manner.

An old man sitting at a café pinches his cheek while he plays cards. From a block away, a middle-aged man sees this odd, seemingly out of place behavior, and a distance of five years is traveled in a matter of one block and a few seconds. A woman confined to a wheelchair would pinch her own cheek and the middle-aged man would see her passing down the hallway now and then when visiting his mother in the hospital. The old man sitting at the outdoor café, pinching his cheek while he plays cards, knows nothing of this memory, and yet he is responsible for the rising lump in the middle-aged man's throat.

The music shifts tempo from a raucous allegro of drums and electricity to the serene largo of a cultivated human voice and a violin. A young man named Martin passes between the crowd of people and (in a gesture awkward for the situation but not unfaithful to his character) puts his arm around the girl's back (she is laughing), and pulls her close to his body. Everyone watches with surprise at what he is doing. The old man playing cards at the café and the young woman with her fingers ascending the escalator have no idea, but Martin knows. He slides his hand into her pocket, finds and squeezes the photograph with all his strength, as if he wants it to disappear between his fingers, and begins painting her portrait by memory.

the portrait

The thin lightnings of blood struck, and a wave pushed gently behind the soft white wall before emerging as a single oblong tear gliding down the crease of her nose. The crowd of people, who had already stopped dancing when they noticed Martin's peculiar gesture, stood silently, reflectively around the girl as if she was a painting hung on the wall of a museum. Martin dropped the crushed photograph onto the floor, leaving it by her feet. He picked up his coat, and left the party as the tear continued to her lip, then vanished into the tip of her tongue, leaving its winding trail behind.

an antidote for roses

an antidote for roses

the smell of roses

The smell of roses reminds me of a funeral. And
although it was the funeral of a man I didn't know, roses
from that day forth insinuated an odor of death that
nauseated me. Recently, I stumbled upon an occasion to
rid myself of that nausea, hopefully forever.

mylene, or a raised eyebrow in contemplation of joy

The leg extending from beneath the café table
belonged to a young woman, who obligingly helped me
to my feet. I saw from her clothes, and from the name
whispered by the label of a beguilingly handsome wine
bottle, that she played at having bad taste. As an apology,
she invited me for coffee; to relieve her of any guilt
unpurged by her invitation, I accepted.

We spoke of nothing in particular, though I let slip
that I was an artist. She feigned disinterest, for I sensed
through dense Gauloises smoke, an undeniable sexual
tension between us that lifted the drowsy eyelids of my
imagination.

After coffee, we strolled leisurely down Boulevard
Moliere and reached a park where I was allowed a few
harmless kisses. As we arrived at the heavy wooden
doors of her *immeuble* numbered 23, she asked if I would
join her for a cup of chocolate in her flat. I kissed her
(harmfully) and suggested that we rendezvous the
following Wednesday at the Hotel Lafayette.

the consolation of a mask

For me, a most compelling justification for marriage is the mischief in which husbands and wives delight at each other's expense. My wife is clever enough, however, to keep her secrets to herself.

But how should I, sympathetic reader, hide from becoming pale or feeling dizzy at the mere sight of a rose? During the days following the funeral, my reactions appeared so extreme to my loving wife that she insisted on psychotherapy. She couldn't understand how the burial of a man I didn't know infused me with such disgust for a harmless flower, arguing that it would have made sense if the person being offered to the worms was someone close to me (a wife perhaps?).

But at that particular funeral of a man I didn't know, death wasn't blurred by melancholy remembrance or emotion. It was death--stark and undramatic--*sans* vanity or ceremony. I had no interest in the dead man, and didn't need or desire the consolation of a mask.

an accomplice of the betrayal

To my astonishment, my endearing wife began taking advantage of my unusual repulsion, presenting me roses after our occasional arguments (as a peace offering), asserting (as the blood drained from my face) that she had forgotten my nausea or that she assumed I was over it. Sometimes I was awakened by petals beneath my nose and had to run to the toilet.

Therefore my scheme's multifarious design--not only to change my memory of roses from repulsion to beauty, but also to exact revenge upon my wife for the past few months of indignity. In the future, whenever she offers me roses, I shall think back fondly of one beautiful night with another woman. My wife will be an accomplice (albeit an unsuspecting one) of the betrayal.

un homme sans-coeur

I overheard (with only one ear) Sabina complaining to her friend a few mornings ago that she was married to *un homme sans-coeur*. I had thrown a rose she offered me through the window, begging a schoolboy on his bicycle to ride back and forth over it.

She said there was only one cure for my recent *misery*: real misery. Her idle chatter is ridiculous, but my condition was becoming unbearable, and I felt more urgency than ever to rid myself of it.

I hurried towards the heavy wooden doors numbered 23, and waited on a nearby bench. It wasn't until evening, however, that Mylene exited, hand in hand with a woman who reminded me of a photographer I once disliked. They kissed (more harmfully than we had kissed), then parted, walking in opposite directions.

I followed the photographer through the Metro, kicking the back of her heels as we exited at Charonne. We reached the Boulevard Voltaire hand in hand, and it might have come to kissing in the elevator if she didn't check her mailbox, making my task easier.

After my brief sortie, I skipped down the street like a playful child, with barely remembered nursery rhymes rolling around the inside of my mouth.

in a state of lowered resistance, the artist is moved

There are certain times in the unfinished symphony that is a life when melancholy chords strike from nowhere, and approach as obtrusive improvisations which (because the symphony is as yet unfinished) seem to have no place or meaning. These are times when I barely know how to respond to a simple greeting, when a falling leaf fills me with apprehension, and I too become capable of being swept away by a breeze, wrinkled by a breath, or drowned by a single drop of rain.

It was during such a moment that I stopped in the middle of the road, asking for silence from the people around me. My flesh sagged on its bones, my heart pumped more slowly, in preparation for a thought.

I thought of Mylene waving to me from an open window as our separate trains pass each other. I suddenly felt that after our single night together, not seeing her again would be painful.

at a glance

I was annoyed by the sudden presence of the photographer in my scheme. But on a rainy day, a broken umbrella once taught me that most situations are beyond man's control, and the sanest thing to do is take comfort in the comedy such situations provide. It was armed with this philosophy that I tolerated the entrance of the photographer in my play. And since the role of antagonist was being capably performed by my beloved wife, I was pressed (as you see, not out of malice or bitterness) by forces beyond my control to limit the photographer's role to that of fool.

"Don't rub the silk for too long and with too much pressure. Catch it at a glance, with a quick stroke of the fingertips," I tell my faithful Juliet. "Then you will experience the sensation of silk."

Juliet never listens to me, and I suppose it is one of the reasons I keep her as a nude model--her playful defiance. She licks the silk with her tongue, and laughs.

I tell her to bring a bouquet of roses to the Hotel Lafayette at eight o'clock on Wednesday evening, and to have them sent to room 2B. She smiles and pulls on my silk underwear, slipping them down to my ankles.

a passing reflection on Sabina

Sabina, the letter 'S' boned away is how I imagine my wife's name on her headstone--even in death something chipping away at her, never allowing her to rest. Part of my infidelity comes from the fact that I know I will never make her truly happy. I see her smile as a thin veil hiding the melancholy of happy moments--a melancholy that whispers in her ear: *this happiness will not last.*

a destroyed face

I exited the metro at Charonne, and sneaked into the apartment of the photographer. (Yes, it turns out that Mylene's photographer really is a photographer.)

In the shadows of the small apartment, I saw a nude black and white photograph of Mylene on the wall. In the shadowed glass of the photograph, I saw the reflection of my face, treated by the dim light with indifference. My face had been suddenly, definitively destroyed in the meeting of light and darkness, and in the middle of that destruction, stretched the naked body of a woman.

I realized I had forgotten what Mylene looked like, and I took the photograph from the wall. I escaped the photographer's apartment, uncertain of what it was I had been searching for.

what i believe in

I was shaken by the image of myself, and was relieved to return home to Sabina, although I wasn't sure what she would do when I burst through the door and ran with my arms wide open toward her. But my nervous gesture (which must have seemed playful to her) affected her in a most charming way. She jumped into my arms, kissing me on my cheek, and for a moment, I recognized the Sabina I once loved.

I felt as if I still loved her, but the passion in my love for her was gone, and only rare moments (with the stars aligned in certain ways, and events such as Venus and Mars affecting the moons of Jupiter) could give us back what we once had. I don't believe in such things, but I do believe in passion.

carmen, or a raised eyebrow in contemplation of joy

Wednesday arrived, and I battled the tourists in Montmartre, where I met Carmen, a sculptor. I invited her to the Musee d'Orsay to see the original *L'Eglise d'Auverse* by Van Gogh. She stood in front of it for an hour, just as I had when I was a child. I wanted to show her my own work at the studio, but it would have been a rushed affair (I prefer a leisurely pace). After all, one shouldn't limit the pleasure one derives from a work of art (whether it is my own, Van Gogh's or Carmen's) simply because the time is lacking. Tomorrow we shall have all day. We made a rendezvous for lunch and kissed--au revoir, a mañana.

I hurried to the hotel, and waited until eight o'clock, but no Mylene. I left, thinking up excuses for her, as I walked home in darkness.

When I opened the door to my apartment, I saw a vase of roses on the living room table. An envelope leaned against it.

Darling,
I am returning to Tours. I never want to speak to you again. Goodbye.

Sabina

If she were sitting in front of me I would have asked for an explanation, but she would have told me I already knew the reasons. The letter in my hand felt heavy and I let it fall to the floor. I touched Mylene's photograph in my pocket, and thought of the broken umbrella that once taught me about such comic situations. Yes, despite the letter, the roses, the dark and heavy silence surrounding me, this was not tragedy--this was comedy.

elephant pieces

elephant pieces

piece i: **the girl appears and disappears**

It had been three years since he'd seen her, and the urgency with which she approached startled him. His hands trembled; drops of wine fell onto the tablecloth.

"Martin," she called to him, and again "Martin."

The splotches of wine settled into the cloth and spread, connecting to form one amoeba-like patch just beyond the outstretched fingers of his fork. The girl disappeared.

Martin realized just moments later that she had disappeared at the instant he began to feel comfortable with her. Those moments, however, were like the passing of centuries, and he tried without success to call her back to him.

Behind Martin, paramedics rushed through the restaurant to help a man who had fallen over. A voice suggested a heart attack. Martin wiped the outside of his glass and tried again to take a sip of wine.

piece ii: **the obituaries**

The obituaries in the newspaper filled two pages that day. A heart attack, cancer, traffic accident, another heart attack, and so on, each of the deceased fitting into one of the different categories.

It was a sort of assembly-line dying Martin thought, worrying that one day he too would fall into the assembly line and have his name printed in a newspaper, his life and death categorized by a few words. The figure of death would ambush him, infect him, then leave him in a hospital bed in a hospital with perhaps a hundred more rooms filled with hospital beds of hundreds of other ambushed and infected people passing their last few days and hours in death's antechamber.

He folded the newspaper in two, letting it fall from his hand into the trash bin, and smoked one more cigarette before limping back to the monotonous work at his desk in the big office, where some of the other workers were dropping torpedoes--pieces of balled up paper--from an opened window. They attacked from the seventh floor and most of their ammunition caught on the wind. Every now and then, though, a torpedo reached its target--a shoulder, a foot, the top of someone's head--and a communal chuckle would precede the next assault.

piece iii: **the virgin**

The full moon lent its borrowed sunlight to the neglected corners of Martin's bedroom. Martin was falling asleep. What if he should die in his sleep he thought? Whether there was a fire in his apartment or his heart just stopped? He would be found in his bed.

The image of a hotel of the dead flashed into his mind, for a bed seemed such a usual place to die, and he realized that his bedroom could have easily passed as a hospital room (as one of those hotel rooms of the dead)-- the walls were bare, and the wallpaper slightly yellowed, not having been changed since the previous owner. He took the pillow from beneath his head, and holding it under his arm, looked out to the moon and the flakes of brown and orange leaves covering the ground beneath their abandoned trees.

There were two, perhaps three uncertain fifteen-year-old thrusts into the girl's recently bloomed opening, the sound of a father's voice, then a panicked burst through the second floor window of the house. It was a good feeling--the jump--until his feet hit the bottom and his legs buckled beneath him in a thudding shock. He had broken his ankle.

Up until that moment, Martin held an uncontested belief of his own immortality. He was convinced that he could somehow survive bullets, knives, fire, being hit by cars (even trucks and busses), and long falls (of which two stories didn't count). He had heard of and seen people hurt and sick, but his own mortality never occurred to him, never became a sublimated feeling until the instant after he heard the crack of bone in his leg. It happened too easily.

When his feet touched down, he rolled with his pillow to break the fall. The memory accompanying his jump was a good and bad one for him--he had lost his virginity, but he had also broken his ankle and was forced to walk with a limp ever since. He had limped through high school, through university, through his job, and he imagined that if he ever got married, he would limp down the aisle as well.

piece iv: **falling**

It wasn't difficult for Martin to remember that day--that particular series of incidents--to separate them from the other images and thoughts in his mind. His lost virginity and a broken ankle.

On that day, what Newton might not have discovered hundreds of years before, Martin certainly could have.

The face of falling was revealed to him, and he had the opportunity to witness another one of its expressions. He had the opportunity to see falling, not just as the force of gravity acting on the earth, but also as an allowing of one's self to be raped by one's own weakness--as a surrender to a more powerful and seductive force.

It was not the father's voice Martin heard that day. He was simply terrified by the novel act he and the girl were committing and lost his nerve to continue. His leap through the window was tantamount to fainting, and his broken ankle only served to justify his wallowing in his own weakness and newly discovered vulnerability.

piece v: **the faces**

The sun looked as if it surfaced from beneath the lake in a slow diffusion of orange light that oiled the water around it. The air was cold. Two men were in a boat fishing.

Martin woke up by this lake to four or five faces he didn't recognize watching over him. He yawned. For the past few weeks, he had awakened to such faces--beautiful faces, ugly faces, ordinary faces. They appeared to him in that state between sleeping and waking he could neither manufacture nor maintain, then vanish.

When the girl appeared to him and approached with her startling urgency, it seemed a breakthrough, for she appeared to him while he was in a conscious state. But that fact, however, didn't seem to help Martin define her urgency or parenthesize it into any concept. She was simply a delicate eruption of memory with no apparent origin.

Martin looked to the boat on the lake. One of the men was screaming and pulling the other from the water. He pressed his hands on the wet man's chest and leaned his ear to his mouth. Martin's eyes retreated from this scene, and rested on one of the faces peering at him. It was the face of a middle-aged man, with streaks of gray starting to show in his hair. His nose was not too large or too small. His eyes were brown. He was wearing a dark blue suit and a yellow tie with blue polka-dots. His shoes were brown.

Martin recognized this memory. It came from one day during the year, perhaps seven--yes, seven years ago, as flakes of snow were just beginning to fall. Martin was waiting for the bus, and this man walked by and asked him for the time. Martin didn't have a watch and told the man he didn't know, he couldn't even guess. It was the first face he recognized.

piece vi: **skipping**

In the backseat of the taxi, wearing his pajamas with his head on his pillow, Martin was going to work. He was fully awake and the faces had disappeared. He looked out to the long line of cars in front of and behind the taxi as they crawled toward the horizon, and watched people walking up and down the street while the driver pressed his horn every ten or fifteen seconds. He put his head back onto his pillow, wondering about this middle-aged man whom he knew for only a few seconds, coughed a few times, then felt a sudden jolt. A car had crashed into the taxi.

Martin lifted his head and looked out again to the long line of cars in front of and behind the taxi as they crawled toward the horizon, and a sudden anxiety gripped him. He realized that he was already on the assembly line, heading to some horizon that would never arrive, that would eventually be interrupted by some unseen, unexpected jolt. His eyes flashed back and forth, then fell, as if the last piece in a puzzle, onto a girl with flowers in her hand, skipping between the mob of walking people, and there was an immediate thinning of his anxiety. Between the flow of people down and around the bent arm of the street, she was a moving pulse. Martin left the taxi, and followed behind the girl with an abbreviated skip of his own. He looked out again to the long line of cars, and pondered the unattractive idea of dying in a traffic accident.

piece vii: the elephants

When the girl skipped in through the front doors of the city's hospital for the mentally ill, Martin did not follow her in. He stopped by the elephant in the window, or rather, he was stopped by the elephant in the window. He walked into the store and his anxiety returned.

The elephants were lined up in rows on a table, and they reminded him of the office where he worked, how the desks were lined up in rows. The tusks seemed to be pens in their penholders, and the ears, sheets of paper falling over the side. Each elephant was made from the same cast, painted blue and black. There was an ugliness about them that annoyed Martin, which he couldn't quite understand, but he left the store with his pillow under his arm and an elephant in his hand.

piece viii: **a playground episode**

The children were jumping from the swings to see who could reach the line drawn across the sand. One tall boy with a new pair of sneakers always did. But it wasn't fair. He was the tallest. The other kids beat and kick him, then drew a new line closer to the swings. They couldn't know that the boy wasn't interested in reaching the line, that he was only interested in the jump--reaching a certain height then falling to the sand. The boy walked home grim-faced, crushing leaves beneath his feet, tossing a baseball up in the air, catching it when it fell. But it became impossible for him to contain his growing anger within the repetition of this act, and he hurled the baseball as far and as fast as he could. When he heard the sound of glass breaking, he momentarily forgot the incident at the playground, and dashed home.

The boy reached his house and ran to the side of his grandfather who was sitting on the sofa. The old man could see that the boy was frightened and held him as best as he could. He tried to reach for the boy's hand, but the boy caught the hand as it was falling and replaced it along with its arm back into the sling. He told his grandfather about the entire episode at the playground, but didn't tell him about the baseball. He wasn't afraid of the kids anymore, only of being caught for breaking someone's window.

The old man replied in high-pitched, confused utterances, and a few nods of the head. His memory was failing him, perhaps had already failed him, and he couldn't even remember pat answers such as "forget it, everything's going to be fine". He just kept nodding his head, and letting out high-pitched words followed by his laugh.   His laugh seemed to shuffle in and out of his mouth, as if it too needed the help of a cane.

The grandfather knew he was forgetting, and understood such forgetting as a sign of his impending death.   There seemed to be only a few memories and images to fall back on now, and he fell back on them like an exhausted man falling onto an old and familiar bed. He would rest on this bed and wait patiently for sleep.

piece ix: **the invitation**

Martin put his elephant by the window and stretched out on his bed. He covered himself with a blanket and began to close his eyes when a woman who had borrowed a purple crayon from him to write down a phone number appeared. He was still in elementary school at the time, long before he walked with a limp.

The instantaneous recognition of this woman and the memory she evoked, was accepted as an invitation by others, and they followed one another from the exaggerated shadows of Martin's room to descend on him...

...a man with a mustache and three lines across his forehead, holding an opened umbrella in his left hand...

...a little girl in green overalls with a button missing on the shirt underneath, patting the head of her little brother, who also had on green overalls...

...an old woman with white hair sitting on a porch getting ready to light a cigarette...

...a woman whose glasses were too big for her, rushing with her dog and a briefcase in her hand, whose arm brushed Martin as he was walking by...

Martin realized he could probably walk out onto the street and see hundreds of people he recognized. Perhaps he could recognize every one of them. It would make sense, after all. Didn't he see hundreds of people in one day whom he wouldn't remember afterwards?

He sat up in bed, thankful that the woman who borrowed the purple crayon from him appeared. The thought of dying in his sleep had become unbearable, and at the time, he was indeed falling asleep.

Martin watched the faces in the silence of his room. He didn't remember that when the girl appeared to him in the restaurant she called out his name. She called to him as if she wanted to tell him something. That was the urgency.

He was just watching the faces come and go and come and go when something crashed through the window and knocked his elephant onto the floor.

piece x: **disappearing**

Martin glued the two pieces together and his elephant was whole again, although it was no longer smooth as it had been before, like all the other elephants in the store-- the thin crack around the elephant's body was obvious because of the excessive glue. But the ugliness that Martin couldn't understand was no longer observable. He held the elephant up to the light. He turned it on its side. He held it upside down. There was nothing to explain it. The ugliness had simply disappeared.

The faces had not.

Martin threw the baseball that broke both the window and his elephant back out onto the grass. He stayed awake the entire night, surrounded by the coming and going faces, and the memories each evoked. As time passed, he began to feel parts of his body disappearing. At one moment, his arms disappeared, next his legs, his neck, and sometimes they disappeared in combinations. He was losing his body in the actions of the people that appeared around him.

In the morning, he looked in the mirror and couldn't find himself. But he saw his elephant. It was in the hand of a man who was wearing pajamas and had a pillow underneath his arm. It must have been him, he thought. And it must have been the sanctuary of routine that took this man out of the apartment and towards work.

piece xi: **the sensation of movement**

Martin's body moved quickly with, through, and between the chaos of people around it. Only the sensation of movement--his arms swinging back and forth, his legs and feet limping and stepping surely then unsurely one after the next, the heaviness of the elephant in his hand, and the delicate pressing of wind on his skin, hinted to himself his own presence. The whole world around him was concrete and glass surrounded by recognizable and forgettable people, and he was part of them.

He felt his legs twisting himself around the usual street corners, the breeze touching the left side of his face, then the right, the cold that travelled with it, closing around him to form the outlines of his body.

"Martin," a voice whispered to him.

The girl with flowers in her hand skipped towards him, the features of her face moving ahead of her body. She whispered as if she wanted no one else to hear.

"Remember me," she said, emphasizing 'me' as if to separate herself from the others.

But the words moved too slowly to reach Martin's ears undetected, and the voices of the other people around him struggled for the same attention. They repeated the two words over and over again until the noise blurred into a hum.

piece xii: **the end**

Martin's body reached the building and he felt his legs climbing the stairs, his hand turning the doorknob of the door to the big office, where some people were dropping pieces of balled up paper from an opened window.

His legs wanted to limp to his desk as they had always done, and his fingers to entwine themselves around a pencil, but Martin stopped himself by the opened window. With this exhausting interruption of routine, he began to recognize some of his features, and he realized that each time he strained against the habitual movements of his body, he became clearer to himself. But it took too much effort.

He imagined that he would go on living like this, with this routine, unable to stop himself from walking in front of a car, or from sleeping, unable to pull his drowning body out of a cold lake, or to dodge the bullets of a gun.

He struggled towards the window, and recognized his legs and the fingers on his left hand. He used his fingers to push his arm through the people, and his arm appeared to him. He was becoming apart from them, and could finally separate himself as his legs coiled then uncoiled, and he felt the rush of wind around his falling body, his fingers gripping the elephant, his ears holding on to the final syllable of a fading echo.

Two pieces of balled up paper followed Martin down, one hitting him on his shoulder. His pillow was soaked with blood, and his elephant broken into twelve pieces.

the mutations, nos. i-xiii:
a universe of dust

the mutations, nos. i-xiii: a universe of dust

a universe of dust

The universe is dead--inorganic rock, uninhabitable planets, chaos--and the living on one planet are only a rare type of what is dead all around. The diseased dead. A mutation conceived by a chance pattern of floating matter in space.

adamania

You shouldn't drink coffee, it makes you suffer. Bishops collaborate with buildings to move against you. Traffic signs break ranks to confuse you into misadventure. You see kisses and memories of Juliet become streetlights of abandoned corners, circling like a carousel.

The moon is drowning over Paris in melancholy drops of rain. Old men playing cards look on as boys curse girls, but the night is polite as ever--paradise.

You're in a room with some woman you don't know, but you think of Juliet--her dress mushrooming above her knees on the windy deck of a ship, and the suggestions whispered from beneath.

Your innocence is diseased. Loneliness in paradise has corrupted you.

pity for the elephant

The bedroom door closes. The piano is alone. You hover the black and white keys like someone who's trampled an elephant in the middle of the road with a bicycle and doesn't know what to do. You play a song you learned as a child, but the notes trip on each other and you remount the bicycle and ride away.

You have pity for the elephant, but it mocks you.

darkbloom

I'm ashamed of you because one of your legs is bigger than the other, though on cold days I don't notice the difference.

a depreciation of the meaningless

Café Zanzibar isn't crowded, but your eyes search the backside of a waitress for the story of your life. A girl leaves her chair and pushes through the door. A boy follows her to the street and a scene is acted out. But the girl's performance is flawed. She has forgotten her lines, and speaks the truth instead. The boy has practiced for this moment and declares that he needs her, that without her his life is meaningless.

truth, or the search for what is familiar

It's raining and streetlamps drip down your window. You look toward the door, hoping for the unexpected arrival, the one truth, the one gripping insight that will help you grow like ivy on an old and sturdy building. But all is hidden from you by the familiar reasons you return to again and again, and your search for the truth degenerates into a search for the familiar.

You hear a noise behind the door, the sound of a window opening, footsteps on the sidewalk. You follow Juliet to Café Zanzibar. She shares a cup of coffee with the redheaded waitress, and a few minutes later, they descend the steps of the Charonne entrance, sneaking like a tongue into the mouth of the Paris metro.

darkbloom revisited

I've come to revel in the extravagance of your leg.

the interrupted cadence

Nothing liberates and ravages the soul like infidelity. The attraction of a hill of dirt, and the sudden silence of civilization. The earth a pebble, heaven a raindrop.

The night is already here mon amie. It arrives without your awareness and hides a danger. Traps have been set and a sinister hum beckons from the darkness--a false comfort—*there is danger everywhere, even in the cup of tea by your bedside.*

But you drink coffee, and walk so slowly that you stand in place for hours before moving to the next bar. A largo. A movement deferred to a bar of a compelling and drunken laughter--an interruption of routine that is a terrifying freedom.

the self, dear brutus, lies not in our stars, but in our faults

Juliet arrives in Copenhagen with a suitcase of clothes. She uses her body for different things and searches for a way to die more stoic than bitter.

Because of her, it's raining in Paris, sharp drops of water that cut your flesh like a scalpel and change the form of your face from one moment to the next. You are never yourself. In fact, you, whoever you are from one moment to the next, no longer believe that this *self* ever existed.

Without Juliet, you have lost that madness that is individually yours. But don't despair. In time you make your loneliness unique, and find your *self* once again. In time, you are nothing without your loneliness.

darkbloom, darkbloom

I cannot speak as to your eating habits, but I should advise you that potatoes are sufficient.

the homeless

There is a woman you love and there is a woman you should love, and the distance between them is as wide as the seven seas stretched beginning to end. A distance the wandering dolphin treats as one home.

Everybody is one home. It is you, the nobody, who is homeless.

suicide

You had your first conception of suffering when you were a little boy. Your father called his mother and told her he was dead. She shrieked so loudly you heard her through the phone, but all the time just the same words from him: "your son is dead, your son is dead".

The buildings are tall enough, and that thought is coming again. The same thought that came for your father. The same thought that helps you sleep at night.

la voix

It has been 109 days since the birth of your loneliness and already it walks into unwelcome places. It speaks out of turn, incoherently, inappropriately. It is misunderstood, and misunderstanding feeds it dreams. In time, it matures into madness and dreams more fantastically. But again mon amie, don't despair, for there is a voice that consoles you: *'Keep your dreams, the wise have none so lovely as the mad.'*

between the last read pages
of an interrupted novel

between the last read pages of an interrupted novel

the quivering nostrils

Martin follows the faint panty lines as they disappear between the woman's slightly spread legs. There is nothing else to do while waiting for the elevator, and he decides he doesn't have the energy to restrain his eyes from supping as indulgently as they wish.

It is Friday, the final day of a miserable work week, and across town in another office building, another man is staring intently at a woman's nose. When the woman speaks, reaching certain inflections, her nostrils quiver. The man is physically excited at the sight of her quivering nostrils and demands half-jokingly that she accompany him to dinner later that evening. The woman says no, and as she says no, her nostrils quiver.

When the image of Martin first came to me, it was with a look of helpless desperation, in an elevator stuffed to near capacity with a woman's backside directly in front of him. With each person entering the elevator, the woman was pushed nearer to Martin until physical contact became unavoidable, and his well-concealed erection became lodged in the subtle rift of her backside.

It is the memory of this embarrassing moment that pins Martin's feet to the floor as the woman enters through the opening elevator doors.

"Aren't you going down?" she asks him, her finger pressing the "door open" button turns white at the tip.

"Of course," he finally answers, shaking his head as if recovering from a momentary spell of dizziness. "I was just lost in thought."

"It was my ass, wasn't it?" the woman questions.

Martin presses the button for the lobby, looks out into the hallway as the doors close, and begins to feel dizzy.

a woman fully clothed

A burst of light ambushes Bernhard's ill-prepared pupils and he throws his arm onto the woman beside him.

"Quivering nostrils," he mumbles.

The words bewilder his drowsy wife and she swings her arm towards him, catching him on his cheek with the pinky and ring fingers of her left hand. Bernhard drops back down to his pillow, and thinks how difficult the night had been, sleeping naked with a fully clothed woman.

the little hairs

As Martin waited for the elevator, his eyes had supped appetizingly enough on the woman's backside, and continuing on an instinctive course, sampled and eventually gorged themselves on those two parts of her body called legs. It wasn't the legs themselves that he found appetizing, but the tiny hairs on the legs. Hairs no more than three or four millimeters in length that drifted back, forth, sometimes not at all, as if only a gentle wave of air, perhaps the breath of a woman leaning over to pick up her fallen hat, had passed over them.

the love letter

On a warm summer day, just outside the Leningrad train station, a woman was whispering to a young man, "Take this letter with you. It's just a love letter. It's for my love. No secrets, you can read it. No secrets."

Markko took the opened envelope and read the address etched on the front. It was addressed to his hometown, a small city near Helsinki.

"Four, five months by mail" the woman whispered. "But here's some chocolate for you. Please take it to him, no secrets."

He placed the envelope between the last read pages of an interrupted novel, and explained to the woman in his best Russian that it was his hometown, and that he would deliver the letter by hand. The woman was delighted, for she knew the train took only five hours to reach, and her lover would get fresh news before he came back to see her. She turned away, leading her bag down the street in a cautious skip.

The train began moving, and the soldiers passed through the cabins checking everyone's luggage. Markko leaned his head against the window to sleep, but the train's repetitive grind wouldn't allow it, and he continued reading his book.

the woman says 'bernhard'

"No," the woman said. "No, no, no, no."

And it was as if Bernhard was in a heaven of quivering nostrils. She had been speaking on the phone at the time, reprimanding or reproaching a colleague about something to do with what was said, or who said what at an early morning business meeting. Bernhard's view to her nostrils was clear, unobstructed, and this sudden eruption of the delicate muscles in and around the woman's nose (the tremors of which Bernhard imagined originating somewhere deep inside her), inspired in him an unprecedented and lasting determination.

"My name is Bernhard," he says later that afternoon. "Bernhard. And I would like to have dinner with you this evening. This evening."

The woman offers him a smile, and leaves a trace of it on her lips.

"Yes," she finally says. "I would love to have dinner with you this evening, Bernhard."

And at no other time had Bernhard observed such delicacy and beauty in her quivering nostrils than at that very moment when she uttered his name for the first time.

the contact

Martin is waiting by the elevator with a wrapped box in his hand. He has seen the woman with the little hairs on her legs three times since their first meeting, but each time he has been frustrated by a different pair of long pants. He is afraid that he may never see her again and decides to make contact with her before the summer is over.

"This is for you," he says, handing a box to the woman.

He glances down at her jeans, and imagines the dark prison, the torture chamber of denim her little hairs have to endure.

"Well, is it my ass?" the woman jokes.

"My phone number is on the bottom of the box," Martin says.

The elevator doors open, but he takes the stairs.

the border

The border between Russia and Finland is an unremarkable landscape, splotched like a pair of painter's dungarees by scattered fragments of wood called houses. But it was this unremarkable landscape that served as the focal point, and the obstacle of the Russian woman and her Finnish lover. It was in the vicinity of this unremarkable border that their lives were being played out.

Markko had stopped reading on page fifty-nine, and it was between pages fifty-eight and fifty-nine that he placed the letter. He held the envelope to the window to see if he could make out any writing on the inside, but he felt sudden pangs of guilt about doing so, even if the woman did say he could read the letter. He decided, however, that his pangs of guilt were actually hunger and he flipped open the flap of the envelope, seeing only the word "darling" before quickly flipping it back closed. He wasn't hungry, after all.

The train continued to grind its way towards Helsinki and the young man carefully replaced the envelope between pages fifty-eight and fifty-nine of his book, then leaned over by the window. He wouldn't have been surprised if the Russian woman's lover was a quite ordinary, unambitious man who would have spent a lonely life if he hadn't met a naive, impressionable Russian woman in Leningrad. The fact that he had a pair of leather shoes--just that he came from outside of

Russia, even if it was only a border away, might have been impressive enough.

the autopsy

"I'll be working late tonight," Bernhard's voice comes through the receiver, and his apologetic tone is satisfactory for his distracted wife. She hangs up the telephone after a quick good-bye, and the wrapped box remains wrapped for only a few moments more after plastic strikes plastic and her husband becomes a mere disconnection. The woman places her new red hat on her head, and takes her blue jeans and blouse off. She walks to the living-room window looking out onto the street, and stands for a long time, stripped of her civilian uniform, with only her white cotton panties, and her new hat on.

"I am Marrikka," she says quietly to everyone who passes within view of the thin layer of glass that stills her image. "My love has offered me this hat."

The sound of automobiles and streetcars penetrate the window, and she walks off to the large mirror in the bedroom.

"Is it my ass?" she asks herself, looking at her reflection.

It has been a long time since Marrikka has undressed in front of a stranger. Only Bernhard knows of the large mole on the left side of her left breast, and the rapidity with which the hairs on her legs grow. She began to feel from Bernhard, however, a certain distance, as if her little imperfections began to repulse him, and she retreated to the security of her clothes, no longer undressing in front of him.

But hadn't she, in fact, recently undressed in front of a stranger, having exposed her "ass" to his imagination, if only jokingly? She had given him permission to cross the denim and cotton borders that separated, disconnected, and protected her from the outside world.

She looks at the mole on her breast and the hairs on her legs. The mirror looks back, much like Bernhard these days, with the cold glance of a medical examiner performing an autopsy, and she rushes to the bathroom before picking up the phone to dial the six numbers on the bottom of the box.

incidental love

I am no longer in love with my wife, Bernhard tells himself as he approaches the woman with a smile. It was as simple as telling Marrikka he was working late and he could do whatever he pleased. She never questioned him. But the aggressive way in which she consented to his secret betrayals annoyed him. Her implicit trust was enough to send his conscience into flights of torment.

But had he, in fact, ever betrayed her? Perhaps in his imagination, perhaps in dreams, but never physically. He never acted on his inner desires. Not because he loved Marrikka, or because she loved him, but because he felt she trusted him and he couldn't betray her trust. Whether she loved him or not was incidental to his infidel thoughts. He could betray her love for him, but he had never gotten so far in betraying her trust, until now.

"Have you been waiting long?" he asks.

"No," the woman says, and her nostrils quiver.

Bernhard takes her hand and leads her to his car.

on marrikka's couch

Marrikka had made a half-hearted attempt at a romantic setting, placing candles on the living room table. But when she opened the door and saw Martin, she felt a strong and sudden urge to throw off her clothes and expose herself to him. Instead, they spent time speaking, exchanging polite conversation, until they somehow maneuvered themselves on the couch.

"The hat looks beautiful on you," Martin says.

Marrikka smiles, and shrugs her shoulders. Martin looks at the long pants she is wearing.

"Would you like to try it on?" Marrikka asks him. She leans over and places the hat on his head.

Martin holds her shoulders and pulls her towards him. He kisses her on her neck, then her cheek, and finally her lips, while his eyes strain to find her legs beneath the cuffs of her pants.

the siren

Martin kissed Marrikka on the mole on her left breast while his hands pulled her pants down. He seemed to smell every scent, the shampoo in her hair beneath the hat, the soap on her skin--and hear every sound, their heartbeats, the distant wailing of a siren, in the moment before he could at last be near those tiny little hairs. He pulled her pants down to her ankles, but he noticed that the hairs were gone.

The sound of the siren seemed to get nearer and nearer, and Martin lost all desire to continue. It was as if something suddenly switched off in him. He picked up the empty box with his phone number and left Marrikka crying on the couch with only the hat on her head, and her pants pulled down to her ankles.

She listened to the siren getting closer, until Bernhard opened the door and the noise blasted into the apartment.

markko delivers the letter

Markko climbed the stairs to the first floor apartment. He was relieved to be back in Finland, back at home, and relieved to be able to deliver the letter for the Russian woman. He took the letter from the book and matched the number on the envelope to the number on the door. He rang the bell.

"There's no one there," a voice came from behind him.

Markko turned around. "Well, it's okay," he said. "I'll just leave it in his mailbox."

"No," the man said. "The man who lived there died of a heart attack. The ambulance took him away last night."

Markko checked the address on the envelope again.

"Yes," the man said. "My wife was terribly upset, crying the whole night about it. We didn't know him too well, but it's always upsetting when something like this happens. Did you know him?"

Markko shook his head. "No" he said. "I didn't."

"My name is Bernhard by the way," the man said, his nose twitching unnaturally. "My wife is so upset about this that she's gone to spend some time with her mother."

Markko thought of the Russian woman, but didn't know what to do. He placed the letter between pages sixty-two and sixty-three of the novel he carried and walked away.

waiting at the train station

Marrikka missed her train, and Bernhard would be calling her mother's house in a few hours to make sure she arrived safely. But she didn't feel like going to her mother's, and she didn't feel like going back home to Bernhard. There were trains going all over Finland, some to Russia, but Marrikka sat on a wooden bench in the train station, and watched the faces of arriving passengers as if she were waiting for someone in particular.

pneumania

pneumania

upstairs in her bedroom

The bed is unmade and I see a long strand of hair on her pillow.

"Those aren't lions," she says.

I watch her lift her arms to the ceiling to touch them. There is something soft in her--something that smells like spring blossoms. And she blossoms before me slowly. So slowly, that I think the universe desires her too and causes the rain that suddenly begins to fall.

music and flying

There is a relationship between music and flying that has yet to be studied. For example, how the arc of a crow's flight influences the texture of a Beethoven sonata. Or how the delicate shifts of a pigeon's wing affects cadence in a Mahler symphony or a Janacek concerto.

In fact, just the other day, Ravel's Bolero was irrevocably changed by the diving of a clumsy pelican.

the bicycle in the yard

The bicycle in the yard is getting wet. The clouds sweep away the blue sky, and she is sleeping.

"I want to tell you something while you are sleeping," I say, "I want to tell you that something has changed. No one can know. The flow of things has changed. This room is different. There is a tension. A feeling, after all. A tension that I want to speak about. A captivating, tangible--yet intangible, movement of some sort. A gripping dementia. A dense impression. A something."

She turns over on her side and wraps the white blanket around her body. The rain falls harder and I imagine her riding a wet bicycle.

"Don't think of things like that," she says. "I don't want to get *pneumonia*."

java

"*Pneumonia*," she says.

Smoke drifts between us, and I wait for a sign--a sea to part, a door to open, a leg to spread.

"Would you like to smell my java?" she asks (I hear a dog barking).

The trumpet player smiles at her when he plays. She smiles back at him. And then I say the unspeakable. Three words that are forced out of my gullet by a geyser of intense emotion. Three words that set me on a course of a subtle, but draining self-deceit: "I hate jazz".

And so I resist the temptation to tap my feet, or to snap my fingers. I sigh. I yawn. I look away and search for the deepest, darkest, most defiled labyrinth of my soul.

friedrich nietzsche and sherlock holmes

"The degree and kind of a man's sexuality reach up into the ultimate pinnacle of his spirit."

So said a great philosopher and psychologist.

"What do you think that means?" she asks me.

"That is a vexed question," I say.

"Vexed indeed," she says. "There are no markings on the original Hung Wu."

It's raining harder, so we stop and wait in the doorway of a sex shop. She smokes a cigarette. In the shop window, rubber penises and plastic women advertise themselves. Across the street, men wander in and out of a private sauna. But in the midst of this suggestive depravity, I try a pure and honest approach, because sometimes even the truth works.

"I like you very much," I tell her.

"I like the big, blue one," she says.

Bilingual prostitutes I think to myself. Are there any? But that's too simple. And then: is there more than one word that ends with the letter v? Down boy, down. Vexed indeed.

mediocrity

I have no talent and therefore I must make due with a common, mediocre soul. And to admit with the little sincerity I have and without pretension, that I desire a simple life and that I am profoundly happy with the little things that I have and with my place in the universe.

"It's not jazz," she says.

And so I ignore distinctions. I ignore the fact that the trumpet player is much more talented than I am. Or that I am slightly more talented than the man who is sitting at the next table. For me there is only genius or mediocrity.

"I'm a simple man," I say. "I don't understand the complexities and nuances of such an esoteric art."

"I'm getting sleepy," she says.

We leave the café. It's still raining and the darker circles of her body reveal themselves to me through her dress.

"The ability to make distinctions," she says, "is a sign of intelligence."

Ouch!

"What's the matter?" she asks me.

"I hurt my foot," I say.

the goose

Of all the birds that affect Chopin, in a positive or a negative way, the goose has the most profound influence. I was listening to Chopin's Variations in B flat, Opus 2 on "La ci darem la mano". Pre-goose, the instrumentation is sketchy at best, the flourishes fall flat, and the articulations are barely perceptible. With other birds, such as the falcon or the parrot the flourishes are lively, but again the instrumentation and overall orchestral quality of the piece disappoints. Only the swan and the duck ((male duck) as they are related) come close to affecting Chopin in the way that the goose does. However, only the goose with its long neck in flight, its webbed feet tucked back, and its grace as part of an entire flock (especially in a bright blue sky) transforms the piece into genius. Suddenly, the bewildering variety of articulation and flourishes are established. The tempest of triplet figurations and decorative variations become magnificent and the cumulative virtuosity of the entire piece is made apparent to even the average listener.

only loved at night

I walk down Istedgade and a woman with bright, blonde hair approaches me.

"Do you want to go with me?" she asks.

"Yes," I say. "Yes I do. But I won't."

I continue down the street as if I stumbled upon a crack on the sidewalk (looking back). A blue light shines on the horizon and a warm breeze blows on my face—a breeze I imagine originating from somewhere between her legs.

"On second thought," I say, "perhaps we could wager a few kroner on a game of backgammon."

"How odd," she says walking towards me, "because I prefer backgammon to chess."

"Is it because backgammon is more like life?" I inquire from the distance.

"Tie me up," she says, still walking towards me. "Yes. Things happen. Logical and illogical. Talent and chance combine. It is an ambiguous world where plans are made and abandoned, and man succumbs to the existential pressure that things beyond his control exert."

"Indeed," I say.

"And then there is you and me," she says stopping in front of me, "you and me. Before money passes hands, and despite the lashes of chaos that strike at us, you and I must smile at the sadistic dominance of one over the other, even say motherly and fatherly words as we resign ourselves to the role of the victor and the vanquished."

We go to her apartment, where I beat her for three hundred kroner.

a mutiny at thermopylae

"If I do something amazing," she says, "a hundred years from now when the story is told, it will be a fairy tale."

The more she drifts away, the more grounded I become, the more concise my desires become. So concise, in fact, that when I speak, whether I speak about the collapse of the Danish empire or about the little boy who was almost run over by a car this morning, that what I want is no longer hidden—no longer protected from the formidable *no*. And so I retreat into a Thermopylae of silence.

However, there is something genuine about desperation, something that defies dishonesty (and silence). And like seamen trapped in the brig of some long barge, my desperation attempts to reach out beyond its purgatory.

"I can't take it anymore!" I scream. "Just give it up! Please! I'm begging you!"

"I think your coffee is too hot," she says. "The glass is cracking."

the dumbest bird in the world

"The trumpet," she says, "is the most beautiful sculpture I've ever seen."

The trumpet player smiles and I sigh.

"This is my pet parrot," he says. "I call him Miles."

Mother of God! I have yet to do research on parrots and jazz.

"Parrots are the dumbest birds in the world," I say (I don't know).

They shake their heads. Ah, the subtly Watson. Only the keenest eye could have detected that. They shake their heads together, and in the same way. I pretend that I don't notice.

"Do you want to come see my band play tonight?" he asks me.

"I don't have any money!"I shout. "I spent three hundred kroner last night!"

the parrot and jazz

It is a commonly known fact that the three most important colors in jazz are red, yellow, and green. Red for bloodlessness. Yellow for cowardice. And green for greedy, grimy, grabbing bastards. And *trumpet* is similar to *trumpery,* which comes from *tromper,* which means to deceive. And that's what those fucking parrots do.

the woman with bright, blonde hair

The Palae Bar is crowded, and I'm waiting in line. I see her and the trumpet player inside talking at the bar. The line moves a little. Now they're laughing, and the line moves a little bit more. The parrot is on his shoulder and she strokes it with her finger. Then the line stops. They're not letting any more people in. And so I stand outside the window of the Palae Bar (clawing, clawing). Not once does she look back. The band is playing and yes—now I do hate jazz.

I leave and walk towards Istedgade. I see a few girls riding their bicycles. It's still raining, and although I have no money, I'm searching for that woman with bright, blonde hair. Maybe tonight, she'll let me beat her for what little I have left.

among the ruins, a trembling rose

among the ruins, a trembling rose

move

It was a day not unlike any other day--the baker prepared the bread at dawn, the bus driver made the left turn at the corner of Rue de Van Gogh at precisely eight twenty-three a.m., the bank president read the newspaper during her lunch hour, and another traveler checked into the only hotel in the center of town.

Martin Martin couldn't sleep. Even with the blinds drawn, the sun still managed to slip into his room, annoying him in the manner a child annoys a parent, and he found he could do little else but embrace the child with an endearing smile.

He thought it strange, his sudden affection for the sun and his compulsion to move. But with each step--from the bed to the door, from the door down the stairs (he didn't even feel like taking the elevator)--the strangeness of it disappeared, and he simply moved without giving his movement any thought.

bicycle

The bicycles were scattered around a dusty yard beside the hotel, some leaning against the rotting wooden fence, and Martin inspected them all before making his final choice (which happened to be the first one he inspected); he marveled at his instincts. There wasn't enough space in the yard to test-ride his bicycle, but he decided not to betray himself by voicing his wish to do so. The day was still light, and he felt he could ride through the small town before nightfall.

still life: lemons

The monkey has learned how to speak, but Professor Wagner does not consider that a success. After all, he once had a dog that almost learned to speak before it was run over by a speeding bus on the corner of Rue de Van Gogh early one morning. The professor didn't make it to the scene in time to hear any last words (if there really were any), but a morbidly curious Madame Bujold (who dropped her bag of lemons to rush to the scene), swore that she heard someone in a low, growling voice say: "it was early".

It would have been humiliating, however, to introduce into society an animal in four-legged trousers that couldn't articulate beyond a low growl. That would have prematurely misjudged the professor and his theory as 'crackpot'. But the monkey was learning quickly and the professor saw only success on the near horizon.

the smell of fresh bread

Madeline found it difficult to be married these days, especially to a man preoccupied with his work. But she had not too long ago found a faithful lover to make her life bearable.

It was lunchtime. She offered a few words to an employee, exchanging a banal memorandum for his newspaper, then walked into her office and closed the door.

She had undressed completely, situating herself on the sofa with a red rose in her hand. The smell of fresh bread filled the bank, as it had often done, moments after she went into her office for lunch.

cemetery

Martin leaned the bicycle against his body and decided to walk it as if he had been riding for too long and his legs were cramped. He found it unbelievable that he had forgotten how to ride a bicycle, but he didn't dare try again. His elbow was bruised, and his body ached from the falls. He wanted to be inconspicuous, and walked toward the cemetery on top of the hill.

It was a quiet place. The stillness of surrounding headstones restrained even the wind, and he found himself calm after the shock of his inability to manage the suddenly strange two-wheeled machine. His eyes moved from grave to grave, reading the dates on each stone as he had often done in his childhood, when he would pretend that cemeteries (with their chipped stones and crumbling mausoleums) were the ruins of ancient Greece.

the cage

They were smoking a cigarette after dinner one evening when the monkey started a conversation (much in the manner that the professor had taught it)

"Professor Wagner," it said. "I have a few questions to ask you."

"Ask," the professor said. "Ask."

"Now that I have learned a great deal from you," it said, employing even facial and hand gestures, "I have no idea what I am to do. What are your intentions for me?"

The professor laughed and drew on his cigarette. He had been expecting this question for some time now, and was pleased that the monkey had finally asked it.

"Well, yes, that is a good question." the professor said. "What you're going to do is to live your own life, be free."

"My own life?" the monkey questioned.

The professor continued, "Do you remember when you first arrived, chained up like a wild beast in that cage over there?"

The monkey simply nodded and the professor inwardly swelled with pride.

"Didn't you wish to be free then?" he asked.

"Yes I did Professor Wagner, and as you can see I have that freedom. I am, after all, no longer chained in the cage," the monkey said.

"Yes, but don't you wish to be even more free? To escape this modest house?" the professor asked.

"At times I do have inklings of that desire, but it is a frightening prospect," the monkey admitted, blowing a ring of smoke towards the ceiling.

"How did you gain your freedom from the cage?" the professor asked.

"Well, from what I recall, I first attempted to break the bars with my hand, something I find completely ridiculous now. I was planning to simply run away from here and go back to the life I had, swinging in trees. But after a few days, realizing the strength of the bars, I began to follow your movements from my cage. I became calmer, imitating you until I attained some manners and I was let out. It was a much easier way to gain my freedom and far less bruising on my hands."

"Then you see, you are already free," the professor said.

The monkey finished its cigarette and asked the professor if he wanted a drink before going to sleep. The professor thanked him kindly, but refused.

9 and a road to the farm

A red crayon escaped the front wheel of the bicycle. It simply rolled out of the way, and Martin picked it up and put it in his pants pocket.

When he was nine, he fell from a tree onto his head. The doctors said if he had fallen at a slightly different angle, he would have snapped his neck and probably died.

What changed the angle of his fall? Was it that another nine year old (born on the same day as Martin) had died, perhaps between the time his foot slipped from the limb and his head crashed into that road leading to his grandfather's farm?

Martin felt connected to this nine year old boy and wanted to place a flower on his grave, but he couldn't find one. In fact, none of the graves had flowers, and he didn't see any flowers in the cemetery.

But he had learned a lesson from his fall. He became more serious, taking after his father, who told him that by the time he was nine, he had already had his own future mapped out, and on his map, he knew where the trees were, and on which trees it was safe to climb.

the lovers

She opened the window in her office, and the baker (her lover) crawled through as he had always done, with a fresh baguette under each arm, kissing her playfully on the top of her head. He was out of breath (having taken a short cut over the hill and through the cemetery) and shuffled to the closet door, unlocking it with a key.

Madeline placed herself on the sofa with a rose in her hand, and her lover (the baker) sat on the floor with his back against her desk, resting the canvas on his legs. He turned over a brown paper bag, spilling crayons onto the floor, blew a kiss to his beloved model and began to outline the curve of her left shoulder.

17 and a woman with red hair

Martin was surprised by how rapidly the sun was going down, but he had found another incidental grave and couldn't turn away. He was still serious at the time, and he was in love with an older woman--a woman whose striking red hair made her unforgettable. When she rejected him, he slit his wrists and his head began floating away.

It could have been this seventeen year old girl who saved him, who floated a few seconds faster than he did; and when she finished the race, the track disappeared before he crossed the line.

Martin couldn't ignore the coincidence of the two graves, a coincidence that struck so quickly it left his emotions numb. He didn't know what to feel, but he felt that he owed those two beings something, that he should thank them for his life. He suddenly felt a terrible fear and wanted to return to the hotel.

contempt

Professor Wagner felt not only with his mind (which he considered formidable), but with his heart as well, that his monkey was ready. Now it was just a matter of assimilating it into society.

"Today, we are going to go for a walk," he told his monkey. "Get dressed. We'll take a shortcut through the cemetery."

The monkey was excited, but contained itself.

"We will meet a few people and speak to them and see how you get along," the professor said.

He imagined giving his speech to other scientists, explaining to the world through television, magazines, and newspapers, what he had come to know as fact: that there is no difference between man and animals. The world would argue bitterly, throwing its own scientific findings at him, but he would have his monkey as evidence.

What made him, however, formulate such a theory? Was it a desire for fame and reputation? Not at all, though he felt it would certainly come. It was his dog. When he learned of that round woman dropping her bag of lemons to rush to the scene of his pet's death, it reminded him of a vulture (the woman was not unlike a vulture in her instincts). The professor formulated his theory and burned to prove it out of his contempt for man, out of a strong desire to leave man dying (on the same streets it had paved) while vultures hovered above.

lost

Martin was lost. It was as if the cemetery had grown in an instant and surrounded him. It became threatening. He turned from one path to the next, but he recognized nothing. He tried the bicycle, only to fall. The sun had gone down and to look into the distance was to look at an endless outline of gravestone after gravestone. What had he done for his two saviors? How had he repaid them? He wandered through the cemetery, until the following afternoon, when he collapsed out of exhaustion.

le nu

The baker turned over the brown paper bag and the crayons spilled out. He didn't have time the other day to finish the drawing (due to an amorous interruption), and once again sat with his back against the desk as the bank president lay naked on the sofa with the rose in her hand.

No one she had ever known had loved crayons as much as he loved them, and it was really this quirk that attracted her. There were others—doctors, salesmen, businessmen, even other bakers that she could have chosen to be her lover—but none of them had ever drawn a picture for her (or of her).

The baker stood up, then squatted down, searching around the floor. He was finished with the drawing, except for the rose, but he couldn't find his red crayon. Madeline put the wilting flower into a vase and pulled her artist onto the sofa. They laughed together at the nude portrait, which made her empty hand (the one supposed to be holding the rose) look as if it were arthritic. They ate their baguettes, then quietly made love.

success

Martin Martin opened a fresh box of crayons, popping one after the other into his mouth, until he finished them. He unfolded the newspaper on his desk, and there on the front page was Professor Wagner. Professor Wagner it seems was insane. No one would believe him when he said that Martin Martin was a monkey. Even Martin Martin couldn't comprehend such a thing any longer, and found it comic (just like other human beings) to see monkeys swinging from tree to tree at the zoo or on television documentaries.

They laughed at the professor, then locked him up. But he could never have foreseen this outcome, especially not after such good fortune presented itself to him on that day he and the monkey took the shortcut through the cemetery.

The body was face down on its stomach and looked as if it were reaching its hand out to something. The professor searched through the pockets (while the monkey spun circles around him on the bicycle), and found a wallet: Martin Martin.

Professor Wagner knew such opportunities presented themselves only once in a lifetime and without giving it much thought, put the wallet into his pocket and began calling his monkey by the name of Martin Martin. The monkey responded (after chewing and swallowing the red crayon it found) quite favorably to its new name.

When the professor finally gave his speech to the newspapers and in front of the television cameras, they laughed at him. Even the monkey had suddenly found him ridiculous and laughed with the others. The only news to report was that Professor Wagner was insane. There was no monkey in the room.

Martin Martin indulged himself, opening another box of crayons, and chewed them one by one, as he finished reading the newspaper.

a trembling rose

Martin had been walking all night and now all morning. The cemetery had become a large, inescapable maze, and he could no longer move. He let the bicycle fall and collapsed. He opened and closed his eyes, then reached into his pocket and pulled out the red crayon he had found. He crawled on his stomach toward a grave, and reached out with his arm. He trembled as he drew the outline of a rose onto the gravestone, then colored it in, before his hand suddenly jerked into a painful, arthritic pose and the red crayon dropped to the ground.

the darkbloom vignettes

the darkbloom vignettes

poetry as suicide

Suicide fouls the air like rotting fish, but Copenhagen is a fishy town. If suicide smelled of roses, or of freshly powdered skin. If suicide was poetry and not piscine...

the surgeon of copenhagen, or le derriere de femme

Juliet stands naked in the middle of my room. I see what is troubling her. She has the ass of a woman who reels against the prism of life—bending fortunes, skewing circumstances, deflecting the image she has of her self away from her self.

I place my hands on her affliction and caress a tragedy here, put the squeeze on a disappointment there, cajole a cathartic confession elsewhere.

sub-terra

It was dinosaur day at the Palae Bar. I ordered a coffee. I smoked a cigarette. I thought about the waitress named Darkbloom. A smile nothing more. On rainy days, she prefers women to men, but the sun was out today. I walked her home and on the way she wept for her deformity, but I was unmoved by her tears. As each fell, a subterranean joy blossomed inside me like a Portuguese woman masturbating in the sun. I fondled her suffering and waited for Hippocrates to slap my hand.

the solitude of misery

Downtown Copenhagen was illumined by a moon that rambled the snow-covered boulevards like the shadow of blackbirds. Darkbloom's naked body danced beneath my window.

There was a time when she was only melancholy and people pitied her. Then she suffered and they passed her on the street as if they no longer recognized her (the broad flat nose, the heavy leg) in search of a more accessible misery.

A giddy nausea overcame me from the sudden understanding of how much she had been spared because of her misery.

I invited her upstairs to my little room. I made her some tea and I asked her two questions.

hell

There is a nightmarish quality to pain. A deep purple vintage. Hellish and beautiful like nightmares are beautiful. Beautiful like hell is beautiful.

Then "drowning, fire, standing on the ledge of a window, a pistol, a pistola, hari kari, kamikaze, a mysterious blue pill that slides innocently down the throat".

"To get to the essence of a thing," she said, "we must understand its beauty. One day I will understand the meaning of everything."

the solitude of joy

Darkbloom has disappeared. Perhaps she has improved, but consequences have been suffered. There were warning signs. The awkwardness that comes with being unhappy. The badly tailored metaphors. The ragged wit.

One day joy will explode in her and shrapnels of joy will pierce the flesh of the mob around her. Every cell in their bodies will quake and they will pass her on the street as if they no longer recognize her and seek the company of a more accessible joy.

the affects of marble on the scientific mind

Marble sepulchers bend between the opened window. The rosebush sighs, the playground mourns—insinuations of what my calculations reveal. But I have instruments that turn spirit into flesh, wine into blood, and the consolations of God into oblivion.

kafka and gogol on the playground

Today is like any other day. The same number of minutes, the de-finite movement of second hands, solitary nights, preparation, a trembling on the verge of erupting into…and then nothing.

The instincts for suffering—the swing of agony, the slide of despair, the cold-blooded seriousness of a child at play—are gone. One realizes that no Kafka played here, no Gogol and that this suffering is not real suffering.

sister miranda of amsterdam

She said that it happened without her awareness—that feeling between her legs. But when she was finally aware of it, she didn't know what to do. She felt despair, and her life became an objection to living.

Sister Miranda was eloquent but incorrect—guilt is killing her. Surgeons like me have a cure for innocence but none for guilt, so all I could do was to give her something to ease her pain: pleasure. I undressed her and placed my hand between her legs.

After some time, her hips lifted slightly and her body trembled. She said a prayer for me, and I told her that if she needed a stronger dosage to visit me again.

The marble garden

When I see a garden I think of you.
The wooden bridge over the stream.
The hanging willows and white marble.
The blackbird and the butterfly.
The reds and violets of roses and violets.
The yearning of branches for another,
And the drifting silence between leaves
That makes silence so palpable.
The playful intimations of rain,
Like the musing whispers
Of a secret love.
And the solitude.

the interrogation, or a letter from darkbloom

Darkbloom wrote thus: $1+1 = 3$ is the mind interrogating itself with intimations of torture at the $=$ sign. The universe is the mind trying to understand itself.

real and the appearance of real

I saw Juliet on the street today. My cure for her seemed to be permanent. Her ass looked fine. She told me that I was in love with Darkbloom, the woman who proved incurable for me. I shrugged my shoulders because you never know who you are in love with and it may have been Darkbloom after all.

She leaned over and whispered to me: "Today is the last day that I see nothing magical in this world. Even my suffering will sparkle and play sleight of hand tricks with me. Rabbits will appear and disappear. Illusion will grapple with reality. My joy will be as painful as my pain and I will see and feel things that people will not believe."

rose enclosed field

I ventured to Café Zanzibar in search of Darkbloom. I saw Sister Miranda sitting at a table by herself. She told me that she saw the waitress named Darkbloom walking down Istedgade with a can of gasoline. She invited me to her hotel room at Rose Enclosed Field #7.

"You are a great surgeon," she said. "You have cured me."

When we arrived at her hotel room, she pulled my pants down and said she was curious about something. She went down on her knees and put her hands together as if in prayer. I looked through the window and trembled, for I mistook wisps of rising smoke for thunderclouds. Sister Miranda satisfied her curiosity and I thought of Darkbloom.

the sadness of the anonymous

A hush when the mob gathered and saw her ablaze. Clouds of black smoke became wings and she rose into the sky. In the beginning, she was mourned by the quiet footsteps behind the trees and the melancholy panting of rain. But it was not the slow motion tumble she had always imagined. It happened suddenly, so that the meaning of everything she had ever done eluded her, once again and forever.

the genealogy of the bicycle, or maria
(a true story)

the genealogy of the bicycle, or maria
(a true story)

Black and enduring separation
I share equally with you.
Why weep? Give me your hand,
Promise me you will come again…

--Anna Akhmatova
from In Dream

the bicycle is a direct descendent
of Napoleon Bonaparte

The Emperor Napoleon Bonaparte often went to his mistress' apartment as what he called a bicycle (the old Corsican word for *secret* or *two wheels*).

'As a bicycle', he often said, 'I can mingle with the common folk and go unnoticed.'

And as a bicycle, he was exiled to Denmark after Josephine mistakenly rode him to the market to buy some eggplants and a chicken. She leaned him against a fishmonger's stand, but his mistress was at the market also and thinking that Napoleon had come to rendezvous, hopped on his back and rode him to her apartment on Rue de Voltaire.

Tragically for Napoleon, Josephine arrived just as his mistress was in the act of dismounting him.

whim and a woman's ass

I'm riding my bicycle along Istedgade and plan to spend the day at the park, reading the collected letters of Napoleon, but I see a woman's ass that makes me change course. And so I wonder if in the *historias brevitas* of this journey that I could have taken a different course that would, in turn, lead to different consequences. But I don't. And that is the dilemma (always in retrospect) that impulse and whim place on a man like me. Could it have been...? Did I...? Should I have...? Perhaps this...? Perhaps that...?

The woman sits at an outdoor café (on that beautiful...), orders a coffee, and reads *the lady with the blue umbrella*. The summer breeze flirts with her hair.

the lady with the blue umbrella

Van Gogh's wheat bends beneath the rain and the lady with the blue umbrella watches dark clouds roll up from the horizon. There is something magical about her umbrella that calms her. Something magical about all umbrellas she thinks—like candles, bicycles, hats, and lullabies. Something that allows them to stretch their wills across generations and even centuries. Something about them that tells her that what *was* still *is*, will never change—and is, in fact, timeless.

from the collected letters of Napoleon Bonaparte
(to Mlle. Maria Elena de A.)

Maria,

...I know that we have held each other before in an intoxicated world that never intersected with this one. But something came back with me the last time we held each other. Something that should be sown in a secret garden and allowed to grow if it will. It is not a convenient thing for us Maria, but it's too precious, too innocent to be destroyed—by me or by anyone...

Napoleon Bonaparte
(Paris, Nov. 1798)

the sigh of the universe

The rain falls and the wind sighs strangely, as if the universe is unburdening itself from a great weight. The woman is eating a peach and I'm thinking about eating a peach too. Thinking of finding a strand of her hair on the café chair. Thinking that I want her to leave something behind. I was happier a few minutes ago. I was happier but didn't know it until now, because I see from the ring on her finger that she is married.

"Is it possible," I ask her, "for two corrupted people to create something innocent?"

"Yes," she says, "but it will happen accidentally, perhaps without the knowledge of either person. Regrettably, however, it will not last. The corruption will inveigle its way into the innocence and eventually kill it. The mere thoughts of the corrupted people will injure the innocence irrevocably. Better not to speak of it. Even better not to think of it."

But I do think of it and I slowly realize that the sigh of the universe is a sigh of regret.

passion

Napoleon placed the blue umbrella against the wall and opened the window to let in the rain. Maria moved to the edge of the bed and lifted her dress to her hips. Then they spoke about the empire, about the meaning of a few paragraphs in a novel, but it was an unspoken eroticism that their friendship was based on.

"If anyone else shares this with you, well then my heart would break into a million pieces," she said.

Napoleon kissed her tenderly. People are corrupt he thought, but passion is innocent.

maria

My bicycle carries me around strange corners and through strange streets, to a park and stops by the woman with the beautiful ass, sun bathing on a blanket.

"You've been thinking about me," she says.

"Yes," I say.

"My name is Maria," she says.

I hope that she has been thinking about me also. Like when she sees a bicycle out of the corner of her eye, or when the breeze blows so faintly that she hardly notices and doesn't know why my face and the indescribable feeling of our first meeting come to her. I hope that invisible forces are at work for me.

"The trees are beautifully silent this time of the year," she says.

I nod in agreement and smile.

"A day can no longer go by that I don't see you," I say.

She takes off her ring and gestures me to lie down beside her. The leaves on the tree above us rustle suddenly. I look up, then look at her, and realize that at this very moment in my life there is no other place that I should be.

from the collected letters of Napoleon Bonaparte

...you are right in saying that we are friends. And yet ours is a friendship that is strange indeed. When you are in the room, I watch you as I watch no other friend. From the very moment that I met you, a strange feeling overcame me, and I wanted to be near you. And now when I am near you I feel an excitement and I want to hold you. Our conversations disguise motives, our glances hide passion. Tell me what this is Maria? Politics and war are easy for me. But this...this confounds me...

Napoleon Bonaparte
(Paris, Jan. 1799)

that is me

Napoleon lifted himself to his full height, and turned towards Josephine.

"I will give you the pleasure of riding me back to the market," he said.

"No," Josephine said, "you are a bad bicycle."

Maria left the room.

"I am a man independent and strong enough to follow this or that impulse no matter where it takes me," he said haughtily, "and to say to the accusers of my indiscretions *so what, that is me. I am Napoleon and there is no other.*"

"You are, of course, correct my Emperor," Josephine said coldly, "but even the strongest man, independent enough to follow this or that impulse is often made a slave by them."

love

Think of it in this way...

You are walking down the street, but before you turn the corner, you can see what is already there: children running across the road, a man asking for directions, a newspaper leaf pausing in the wind. And then you turn the corner, but you see Maria waving to you from the distance, and a black bull chasing a cabaret dancer along the sidewalk, and a scarlet flag covering the sky. The statues in the park are sunlit bronze, the grass is green, and a bicycle leans against the spitting fountain...

maria, whispered

When I wake up, I am on my bicycle. It takes me from Copenhagen through the Danish countryside. I pass farmers in Germany. Day turns to night. Night turns to day again. I sleep. I wake up. I yawn and stretch. I think about the hundreds of years that the trees have lived—lived in front of the houses that have been built, destroyed, and rebuilt. Kept every secret, even those of the most reviled men, and whispered nothing, not even to the wind. I say Maria's name silently to myself—*Maria*. And again, *Maria*. Then thoughts about her and her husband, living in the same house, sharing the same bed make my bicycle race faster and faster.

Such pain, I think. How is it possible that anyone could endure such pain?

from the collected letters of Napoleon Bonaparte

Maria,
...this is my last letter to you. And this is what I want to tell you...that I will always think of you from time to time. That I want nothing from you that you will not give of yourself freely. That our friendship is rare. Rare in its intensity if not its duration. There is more that I should say, but there is a certain incommunicability of the heart. Something transparent, yet deep. You do understand. Maria, think of me from time to time. Think of me now that I am no longer Emperor...now that I am but two wheels, a broken bell, and a scrap of twisted metal...

Napoleon Bonaparte
(Paris, Mar. 1799)

a letter to napoleon

I arrive in Paris and my bicycle stops in front of an apartment on Rue de Voltaire. I climb the stairs and open the door. I walk past the hallway into the living room. I pull up the rug and remove a panel from the floor, where I find a letter written by Maria Elena de A. to Napoleon Bonaparte dated March, 1799.

Cher Napoleon,
My heart is broken and I am damaged beyond repair without you. I will look for you and promise that I will find you one day. Two souls such as ours shall always find each other...

I think about Maria. Outside it begins to rain. A lady with a blue umbrella passes by the window, and my bicycle leans against the oldest tree in Paris.

the etymology of the Swedish Queen

the etymology of the Swedish Queen
by
Alón Elymadma Niñoz
*(dedicato alla Regina di
Sverige)*

*translated from the Italian
by copernicus de savinien*

belladonna

Before I begin this story, I want to say that I'm
watching you two. Watching the way you lean towards
each other while you speak about the most innocuous
things: tomatoes, weather changes, shoes.

I knew a thing or two about tomatoes at one time.
For example, the fact that they are a genus of the
nightshade family, which includes potatoes and
eggplants, not to mention several poisonous weeds.
But now I have forgotten. As for weather changes, I
know only that the two words *climate* and *climax* come
from the same Greek word *klinein (to lean)*.

Shoes, of course, represent the female genitalia.

desire

A word or two about desire. Please pardon this
digression. Bear with me.

Desire comes from the Latin word *sidus* that means
star. And this is how I believe it came to mean what it
means today:

The first man who compared a woman's eyes to those mysteries of light that only showed themselves during the night, and at a great distance, forever connected the word desire, first and foremost, with woman. Throughout the centuries, as the stars became less of a mystery and as mankind moved closer to them, the true meaning of the word became diluted. But desire, as it originated, meant a secret and distant longing. Under cover of night, hidden behind a tree or secluded in the dark entrance of a cave one could *desire*.

But although the stars are no longer a distant mystery to man, woman still is, and therefore the true meaning of the word, although it has become misused, is essentially unchanged.

a brief study of *moments*

The truth and beauty of things can only be grasped in moments. In fact, the only reason that I could write a story about you is because I caught you in a moment. A moment that touched me in such a way, that I wanted to hold you. But moments are, of course, fleeting--

Let me rephrase: *the truth and beauty of things only show themselves in moments.* I am, of course, foolish to say that moments can be grasped (forgive me). Because they leave a trail that can't really be followed. We try to find our way back to them through different things such as art or love, but they are impossible to return to. We can never really capture the original moments; only a kind of mutation of the moments, and so it adds a melancholy to them and perhaps makes them seem more beautiful than they really were.

With this in mind, I hope the story that I will tell seems more beautiful than it really is.

a dog in the night

You torture me with the most simple acts. If it rains, you open your umbrella. If it's hot, you take off your sweater. Then there is the smell of you. Am I a dog? Am I the only one who smells you when you are in the room? Hear me in the night, howling alone in the kitchen. The floor is cold, but I, who feel so much, cannot feel it. And what am I howling? Your name, no doubt. Just to say it. Just to whisper it from time to time to myself. To sprinkle it into the middle of a conversation for no reason: "The philosophical position of the Parliament--Maria..."

the moment

Oh yes, the moment. Let me try to describe the moment that inspired me to write the story you are about to read:

It was late morning, after the rain. The sun was shining and I was looking through the bedroom window. Looking through the bright green, wet leaves of the tree. You rode your bicycle into the yard, leaned it against the gate, and ran into the house.

analysis of the moment

It was late morning, after the rain.
Only when you are by yourself are your actions pure.

The sun was shining and I was looking through the bedroom window:

My own eyes (the mere act of looking at you) cast a penumbra around you and began to make you vague to me.

Looking through the bright green, wet leaves of the tree:

I tried to see you more clearly by focusing on your body.   To focus on your face, your breasts, your shoulders...

You rode your bicycle into the yard,:

I wanted to hold you.

leaned it against the gate,:

I wanted to make love to you.

and ran into the house,:

Quickly you became part of my thoughts. Occupied that part of my brain that longed for beauty and poetry.

the last time i saw you

We could have kissed for a few minutes more. The door was closed and they were inside talking.   And night would have kept our secret, because it was night that brought us together. Then I would have told you everything. Then I would have told you that I... But now those minutes have turned into hours and those hours into days.   And those lips are speaking to someone else--kissing someone else. A few minutes more and I would have told you everything.

watching you without me

There was a hole in your bedroom wall and I looked through it. I watched you undress and put cream on your face. You walked into the bathroom and I heard you brushing your teeth. What was I watching? You bent over and scratched your ankle. You brushed your hair.

I am ready to never be with you again. Just a murmur of agony in the place you once stood. Just a shudder of pain at the passing of a familiar scent. You will go out into the world without me and make it your own. You will collapse into the arms of freedom (your true love) and regret nothing.

why you do not love me

Men like me are never happy. But that is nothing to pity because we withdraw from this happy world with alarming ease. You say that the walls in my little room are bare, like the madman's at the asylum. And I say to you that my paintings hang on the walls of my soul. And my books sit on the shelves of my soul. And my music plays in the arena of my soul. So pardon my silence—my disinterest in what happens around me— my blank demeanor.

You say that I am heartless. And I say to you that my heart too, resides in the cavern of my soul. And though no one knows it, that is where you are. That is where you will always be.

a blown away leaf

a blown away leaf

a butterfly

The barking of a dog strays above the ruins; an acorn trips down the windshield, and Martin opens his eyes, peering at the chipped black silhouettes over the wall. The body beneath him has no name as yet--she is as much a stranger to him as those fleshless bodies rooting the concrete slabs that serve as landmarks of the dead.

He pulls up his pants, and the young woman beneath him slides her hand between her legs. He turns over, settling into the driver's seat, starts the engine, and drives off as she masturbates beside him. The fragrance of flowers in the backseat lingers above the unblushing aroma of her sex.

At an abandoned intersection, Martin stops the car and gets out. He hops into the air, then down, then up again, and with a butterfly's innocent disdain for gravity, floats away into the night. Everything is wet; drops of rain appear to be falling light, each carrying inside its opalescent body, tiny pieces of the moon and the stars.

a caterpillar

A Parisian train station sidewalk. In the distance, the chugging of winding caterpillars evaporating in the misty morning of a Paris that wakes up. A man, a bouquet of flowers in his hand, kisses his wife gently on her cheek.

The wife presses the bouquet to her chest and climbs aboard, waving good-bye from the window, watching her husband become smaller and smaller, until he finally disappears as the train maneuvers a bend in its tracks.

"Ticket, Madame," the porter says opening the door to the cabin, and Madeline obliges.

The young woman sitting across from Madeline searches through her clothes and bag.

"If you don't have it, you'll have to pay the seventy francs," the porter says.

The young woman says nothing. Madeline gives the porter a hundred franc note.

The young woman looks down at her worn shoes; a whispered "thank you" passes from her lips.

kangaroos

Edwige was sitting on a wooden bench in the square behind an old abandoned church, reading a very thick novel--Oneypa Paya's (the father, not his scandalous junior) magnum opus *Don Quixote's Map of the World*--and three children hopped noisily toward her.

"Madame," one of them asked, "what are you reading?"

Edwige turned the book over onto her lap.

"My curious little kangaroo," she answered. "I cannot possibly read for the moment because you hop too loudly."

The three children laughed (and Edwige too), and pretended to speak quietly as they hopped around the square and finally away. There was probably a time Martin thought to himself as he watched the scene from his car, when the old church was surrounded by endless, uncluttered land. He imagined that as the children grow into their adult bodies, they will begin to feel trapped by them, the square will no longer be large enough, and they will have an unconscious longing (an irritating itch in the brain) to hop around in a vast open space. Martin watched the young woman on the bench, and tried to imagine himself as one of those children looking at her naked body.

a reflection

The young woman settles back into her seat and leans her head against the rattling window. She watches Madeline's reflection in the glass (a pastel-like transparency against the passing landscape) and wonders if Madeline has noticed their resemblance. It was an image of herself the young woman could never have imagined: sitting with her legs crossed, her fine leather shoes, her rose patterned spring dress, her bouquet of flowers, and her book (the same novel by that suddenly celebrated Spanish novelist Señor Oneypa Paya).

"Are you feeling well?" Madeline asks.

The young woman straightens herself.

"Ah, yes Madame," she says.

"Madeline, my name is Madeline."

The young woman lowers her head slightly, "Thank you again for--" she begins.

"--it's nothing," Madeline says.

Madeline flings the book into the seat beside her. "It's quite dull" she says, "I find his son's work far more exciting. Are you going to Orleans?"

The young woman nods her head.

"Your family is there?"

"Yes," she says. "My parents live there."

floating

Martin watched Edwige pick up her bag, put her book into it, and walk away. He recognized her walk. It was the walk of someone who had a destination, a home perhaps. She didn't shuffle along unsurely, but moved with unthinking faith in gravity, so that if the moment came when neither foot touched the ground, floating away like a leaf wasn't even an unconscious possibility for her--her feet would brush down with a delicate certainty.

Driving away from the small town, he wished now that he had spoken with her. He stared at the road ahead of him, looking for a sign to Paris.

an urge

The drunk foreigner (his accent sounded German) enjoyed the use of her hands without putting any francs in them. He ran off and left her crying in a doorway with her saliva-stained breasts hanging inside her opened shirt.

When the young woman decided to take the train away from Paris, she didn't know where she would go--just away--but she could never have imagined meeting her double (she could say that they were twins). She felt frustrated that Madeline didn't seem to notice.

"You look like my sister," the young woman says.

Madeline glances over her book. "Your sister is in Orleans also?" she asks.

"Yes," the young woman says. And for a moment, she feels as if Madeline recognizes their resemblance, but Madeline's eyes fall back to her unfinished sentence.

The young woman has an urge to put her arms around Madeline, kiss her, feel her breasts. She crosses her legs like Madeline's and flips her hair towards the left side of her head. She even begins to play with the earring in her left ear (although she doesn't wear one) in the same manner that Madeline plays with her own.

climbing the church in copenhagen

The spiral staircase around the outside of the church in Copenhagen curls around the tall steeple in the wrong direction, counter-clockwise. The architect, having been made aware of his blemish, climbed the stairs to the top of the steeple, then jumped, killing himself.

In a house a few blocks away, a boy was looking through his telescope at the moon and the stars when he noticed the man leap over the railing. The man was looking at his church, a strange look of desperate indecision, and for a moment, he seemed to float on a wave of air. But just as suddenly, his eyes closed, his face twisted, and his body slammed into the ground.

No one believes the boy about the man's moment of hesitation in the air. But Martin does. He believes it was a moment when the uniqueness of the architect's creation seemed wonderful to him, and was inspiring. But this very same uniqueness--this one in a billion--spawned an unbearable desire for fraternity, and weighted his body, hurling it mercilessly towards the ground.

madeline

The train stopped, and Madeline closed her book. They had arrived in Orleans, and the young woman was disappointed that the trip hadn't lasted longer. She was thinking of asking Madeline to lunch, or for coffee in a café.

"Your family will be here to pick you up?" Madeline asks her.

"No," she says, looking at the emptiness of the train station. "I don't live far from here."

"That's good," Madeline says.

"Do you have any sisters?" the young woman asks.

Madeline shakes her head, "No, I don't," she says.

They step from the train together.

"By the way, what's your name?" Madeline asks.

The young woman looks back toward the train.

"My name is Madeline also."

Madeline smiles.

"Take these for yourself and your family."

She hands the young woman her bouquet of flowers, says good-bye and turns to leave. The young woman stands without moving, her bag over her shoulder, the bouquet of flowers cradled in her arms, and watches Madeline until she can no longer see her.

"Madeline," she says quietly to herself, pressing the bouquet of flowers against her face.

the fragrance of flowers in the backseat

The sun is going down, and Martin is on his way to Paris when he sees a young woman walking along the highway with a bouquet of flowers in her hand. He passes her, but continues to watch her in the rear view mirror. It is a strange sight--a young woman walking along the highway with a bouquet of flowers in her hand. He pulls over to the side of the road and waits for her.

The young woman steps into the car. She crosses her legs, flips her hair to the left side of her head, and plays with the earring in her left ear (although she doesn't wear one). She places the bouquet of flowers in the backseat, and quietly whispers the name Madeline to herself over and over again as her hands pass over her face and down to her breasts. Martin imagines her naked. An orange glow lingers above the horizon and drops of rain begin to tap against the body of the car.